THE CHRISTMAS CAT

THE
CHRISTMAS
CAT

Robert Westall

Illustrated by John Lawrence

METHUEN CHILDREN'S BOOKS

Also by Robert Westall,
available from Methuen Children's Books:

A WALK ON THE WILD SIDE

THE KINGDOM BY THE SEA
(Winner of The Guardian Children's Fiction Prize)

IF CATS COULD FLY . . .

First published in Great Britain 1991
by Methuen Children's Books
A Division of Reed International Books Limited
Michelin House, 81 Fulham Road, London SW3 6RB
Reprinted 1991
Text copyright © 1991 Robert Westall
Illustrations copyright © 1991 John Lawrence

Printed in Great Britain by St Edmundsbury Press
Bury St Edmunds, Suffolk.

British Library Cataloguing in Publication Data

Westall, Robert 1929–
The Christmas cat.
I. Title
823.913 [F]

ISBN 0 416 16822 1

for Caroline Walker
of Stockton Heath

Contents

CHAPTER ONE

A Cold Welcome

Granddaughter, I was once as young as you. My legs were as long and thin and could run as fast. I could climb a wall better than any boy, even when there was broken glass on top. And my glory was my red hair, so long that I could sit on it.

That was the year 1934, my parents were abroad, and I spent Christmas with my Uncle Simon. My Uncle Simon was a vicar. Vicars then were not like vicars now. If you know any vicar now, he is probably a young man who dresses in ordinary clothes, and tries to make friends with everyone, even if he has a rather desperate smile and a rather uneasy laugh. Vicars are a threatened species now, and they know it. Soon, there may be hardly any vicars left, and some will be young women.

But vicars then . . . they had the *Power*. They dressed all in black, and people were rather afraid of them. I have seen a vicar empty a railway carriage, just by sitting in it. Just being there, they made people, ordinary people, mums and dads, aware of their *Sins*. They made them feel feeble and wicked and helpless. So people avoided them if they could.

I did not want to go to the vicarage for Christmas. I would rather have stayed on at school, with the headmistress, who was a good sort. But my father had written: 'You must go and stay with Uncle Simon. He has asked for you. Perhaps you will be able to cheer him up.'

I had doubts about cheering myself up. Uncle Simon had no wife and no children. The family said he had given himself to God. God did not seem to have made a good job of cheering Uncle Simon up. Uncle Simon always sent dark small miserable Christmas cards with *Holy People* on them, that wished you a 'Blessed and Peaceful Christmas-tide'. I much preferred Santa, grinning with a sackful of presents.

Still, off I had to go, with my whole school trunk, and a purseful of silver sixpences, to tip the railway porters.

All I knew about North Shields, when I arrived that Sunday, was that the people there made their living from fish, and I would have guessed as much as soon as I put my head out of the railway carriage. There was a mountain of kipper-boxes on the platform, and the smell of kippers would have knocked me flat, if the smell from a mountain of dried cod-boxes had not pushed me the other way. Outside, the cobbles of the taxi-rank were stuck all over with tiny silver scales, and the air was thick with the smell of fresh fish, frying fish, rotting fish, boiling fish and guano. Seagulls sat on every rooftop, nearly as big and arrogant as geese, and splattered the slates with their white droppings and filled the air with their raucous cries.

When I gave the taxi-man the address of the vicarage, he stopped being jolly and friendly, and went all quiet, as if I, too, was dressed all in black and had a huge Bible in my hand. We drove through the town. Every street-end gave us a view of the river with its mass of moored boats. The men and women looked strange to my southern eye;

the men in huge caps and mufflers, the women in black shawls. There were shops, but most people seemed to be buying stuff off little flat barrows. There were no cars and lorries, but a lot of horses and carts, and the cobbled streets were thick with flattened masses of horse-dung, looking a bit like big round doormats.

'Here's the vicarage, hinny,' said the taxi-man, pulling up with a squeak and a jerk. I saw a great high, black brick wall, with broken glass set on top in concrete. Tall, shut green gates. And dark trees, massing their dull green heads over the wall, like a curious crowd.

'That's a shilling, hinny,' said the taxi-man, putting my trunk on to the pavement. Then he added, doubtfully, 'I hope you'll be all right,' and drove rapidly away.

I stared at the wall and gate aghast. It looked like the wall and gate of a prison, or at least a home for naughty children. The gate looked as if it was locked; but I managed to wrestle it open, and saw a short weedy drive leading up to a house that might have been pretty, except that the smoke and soot of the town had painted it black, too. I dragged my school trunk inside, and closed the gate

and went and knocked on the door of the house. The knocker gave a terrible boom that seemed to echo in every room inside. It seemed to make a noise that was far too important for *me*.

At last, the door opened. The woman who opened it didn't see me at first; she was looking over my head. Then she looked down and saw me and said, 'The vicar's out.'

'But,' I said.

'But nothing. The vicar's out. He's down at the church if you want him. Saying Evensong. I've nothing for you here.'

'But . . .' I said again.

She'd closed the door in my face.

By this time, I was close to tears but I'd long since learnt that tears don't get you anywhere. So I sniffed them back, and went to look for the church.

There were plenty of people around, but I didn't know who to ask. They were such a strange crew; Blacks and Chinese with pigtails, even the men. Groups who looked like Indians, only they wore rags round their necks and suits of thin blue washed-out cotton, and talked at a great rate in their own language. Men who might have been Spaniards, with gold earrings and thin moustaches and flashing smiles; and men who might have been Germans, with cropped hair, and a stolid unsmiling way of stumping along. Even the women talked in a strange accent, though you could pick out the odd English word.

Then I saw this ordinary man ambling towards me. He seemed to be slightly ill, for he swayed as he walked, and wobbled across the pavement, several times nearly falling into the gutter. But he had a nice face, and was smiling to himself. An unbuttoned sort of man; an unbuttoned overcoat over an unbuttoned coat, over an unbuttoned waistcoat.

'Please could you tell me the way to the church?'

He looked at me like a wise owl, and the smell of his breath was worse than the fish. Whisky. I always hated the smell of whisky. My father sometimes drank it, in the evenings, and I would not kiss him then.

'Aye,' he said, 'but which church? Are you a damned Papist, or a damned Nonconformist, or a True Believer?'

'Sir,' I said, looking him straight in the eye, so that I made him sway a good deal more. 'I am a True Believer!'

15

'God bless you, hinny,' he said, tears springing into his watery blue eyes. 'Ah'm a Sinner, a Terrible Sinner. It's the drink, you see. Ah drink and then Ah do terrible wicked things . . .'

'The church,' I said, as firmly as possible.

'Ah'll show ye.' And the next second, he had enclosed my hand in his huge warm dry one, and was leading me a staggering dance

along the pavement, still telling me of his
wicked sins, though not in any detail, which
might have been interesting . . .

'There's the True Church,' he said at last,
pointing. And I had no doubt it was. For it
was as black as coal, and the door was
barred by huge rusty iron railings, and a
black notice board announced Uncle Simon's
name in small gold Gothic letters.

I thanked him; but he would not let go of me; he kept on going on about his sins. At last, I had a brainwave.

'Come and see the vicar. He's inside. He's my uncle. He'll help you with your sins.'

'God forbid,' said the man fervently. 'My sins are too black for any vicar to help.' And the next second, he was gone.

The rusty gate was not so fortress-like as it looked. It opened under my hand. So did the great studded door. I was in dimness, with the saints staring down at me, all purple and red and blue, from out of their stained-glass windows. There was a smell of polish and Brasso and incense and dust and mice.

And the sound of my uncle singing. He had a very beautiful voice; his voice was the only beautiful part of him. He was singing half the service, and a cracked old voice was singing the other half.

'O Lord, open Thou our lips.'

'And our mouths shall shew forth Thy praise.'

'O God, make speed to save us.'

'O Lord, make haste to help us.'

I sat, and listened to the end. I listened to that lovely voice preach about the feeding of the Five Thousand. He preached very well.

The only thing was, that apart from me and the old lady at the organ, the huge church was completely empty.

'You walked down here by *yourself?*' said my uncle. 'You must never do that again. I cannot imagine what Mrs Brindley was thinking of, letting you come down here by *yourself.*'

He did not look at me. He looked at his pulpit, at the board that gave the numbers of the hymns, at the saints in the stained glass

windows. Never at me. Not all the time I
stayed with him. I got the feeling, in the end,
that I was accompanied by an invisible
person, two feet to my left, that my uncle
talked to all the time.

'Why not?' I asked, greatly daring.

'Child! This town is filled with such
wickedness that your poor young mind could
not contain it. You cannot breathe the air of
these streets without being defiled. Such
sins . . .'

But he didn't go into any detail, which
might have been interesting. Just like the
poor whisky-man . . . My mind went over
the wickedest things I knew. Which were
not very wicked in those days,
granddaughter. I have learnt a lot since.

'We must rescue your trunk. Before they
steal it.' That at least made sense. We'd had
thieves at school.

Together we hurried up the road. A way
cleared before us, through the milling crowd,
as if by magic. A lot of people actually
crossed the road to avoid us.

My uncle seemed surprised to find my
trunk still lying where I had left it. He picked
it up with a grunt that made me worry for
him. He was older, much older, than my

father. He had silver hair; and an old cracked broad leather belt, round his long black cassock, that strained at the last hole. Tall and portly, my uncle was.

Mrs Brindley opened the door to his knock, undoing both the top and bottom bolts with a rusty squawk.

'Oh, it's you, Vicar! Is this young woman pestering you?'

'Of-course-not,' gasped my uncle, lifting my trunk again. 'She-is-my-niece-my-brother's-daughter-that-I-told-you-of.'

'Oh,' Mrs Brindley looked at me; for the first time, really. There was a certain amount of curiosity mixed with her hostility.

'Well, I only hope she's not too much for you, Vicar. You've got so much to do, and so have I.'

Such was my welcome at the Vicarage.

CHAPTER TWO

A Pine Cone in the Ear

I spent three days of sheer misery. It was not that my Uncle Simon was at all a cruel man. He simply forgot I existed, unless I reminded him, and then he did not know what to say to me, and there were long terrible silences, especially at mealtimes.

I certainly wasn't starved. Meals were the one way Mrs Brindley spoiled him, and he ate a lot, and I ate a lot, too. It helped to fill up the silences at mealtimes. Real heavy stodge it was; worse than school.

But I was so *cold*. The vicarage was huge; like a great polished refrigerator of dark wood. My uncle had a fire in his study during the day; but I was forbidden to go there, in case I disturbed his reading. The only other warm room in the house was the kitchen, and that was Mrs Brindley's lair, and she hated me. She thought she owned my uncle, and I think she saw me as a rival.

I couldn't even stay in bed to keep warm; I tried that once, and Mrs Brindley soon rooted me out. Staying in bed during the day was sinful, and she had a terrible nose for sinfulness, like a bloodhound.

No, I must go out and play. Only when I went outside could I wear my coat and beret and scarf and gloves. Wearing them indoors was also sinful for some reason.

So I went out. Not, of course, out of the green gate into the sinful town. I soon learnt that Mrs Brindley kept a keen eye on the gate; I was even accused of going too near it, of *thinking* about going through it. No, I was confined to an acre of woodland, inside the high wall.

Woodland? It was ornamental trees of the darkest, most hideous sort. Pines and firs and monkey puzzle trees and holly bushes grown five metres high, with nothing but pine needles in between. And wretched dark rhododendrons. It couldn't even boast a bird, let alone a squirrel.

There were the old stables; they gave me a happy hour, exploring, for they had only just been abandoned. Harness still hung in the harness-room; there was still staw and hay in the stalls, and even a pony-cart with its spokes loose with damp and its tyres red with rust. I thought of lighting a fire in the little grate in the harness-room; but I knew Mrs Brindley would soon spot the smoke from the chimney.

But it was there that I made my first
friend. An old black and white cat with long
thin legs and a bulging belly. She was
terrified of me at first; but I had patience,
and all the time in the world. And she was
hungry, so hungry, and I got into the habit of

smuggling an old cloth pouch into the dining-room, in the pocket of my cardigan, and popping titbits from my plate into it. My uncle never noticed; most of the time he was lost in his book at table; though my parents had always said reading at table was very rude. But I had to be careful when Mrs Brindley was about. Still, it was my first defiance, and my first victory.

My second victory started like a defeat. I was wandering aimlessly through the wood, by the high wall at the back, when a pine cone hit me sharply on the nose. It really stung; my eyes filled with tears. When I had wiped them, I stared around, but there was nobody about. I thought perhaps the pine cone had fallen off a tree; but as I was thinking that, another hit me on the ear.

I whirled round; no way had that one fallen off a tree. Again, there was no one to be seen. But I noticed one place where a dense holly tree grew up against the wall. It was the only spot in that dreary place where anyone could hide. I went on as if aimlessly wandering; but now I picked up the odd pine cone as I went, choosing the wettest and heaviest ones and pretending to examine them with interest.

When I had about ten in the pocket of my coat, I heard a third missile land in the pine needles behind me. I spun quick as a flash, and saw the holly tree move, and threw my heaviest cone as hard as I could. Then another, and another. I was no mean shot at throwing a cricket ball, and now I could see a vague shadow through the dense leaves. My fourth pine cone hit the shadow. The shadow said 'Ow' in a loud voice.

My fifth cone hit as well; and my seventh. There was a frantic scraping of feet on the wall-top; then a smashing and crashing that carried on all down the tree. Something hunched-up landed at the bottom, on the dead dry holly leaves.

It was a boy, about eleven, my own age. He hugged himself and glared up at me.

'You silly tart! You've broke my leg.'

'You started it!'

'I didn't break *your* leg.'

'Let's have a look at it.' I started forward, a bit worried.

'Gerroff me.' He jumped up so quickly I knew his leg wasn't broken, though he was limping quite badly. He walked up and down, like a footballer who's been hurt, trying to walk the pain away.

'I can't climb the wall like this,' he stormed.

'Then you can go out of the gate . . .' I was glad he wasn't badly hurt.

A look of terror came across his face. 'The vicar will catch me. He'll fetch the poliss to me. For trespassin'.'

'I'll say you're with me.'

'You're trespassin' an' all.'

'No, I'm not. I'm the vicar's niece.'

He eyed me with fresh horror, and turned and made a frantic attempt to climb up between the tree and the wall. But three feet up he stopped, grimacing with pain.

'I'll give you a leg-up if you like,' I said. And went and pushed up on his bottom until, with a terrible struggle, he made the top of the wall. 'Can you manage now?'

'I can drop down. I can crawl home. You can crawl even with a broken leg,' he said bitterly.

Suddenly I didn't want him to go. So, greatly daring, I said, 'I'm not Frankenstein, you know.'

'No,' he said. 'You just look like him.'

I got one of my last pine cones out of my pocket . . .

'O.K.,' he said, putting his hands in the

air, like somebody in a cowboy movie. 'I surrender.' He grinned. He had rather a nice grin. It went with his snub nose. And his blue eyes were suddenly merry. 'You're not Frankenstein. Frankenstein wouldn't dare push a boy up the bum.'

'I'll come up,' I said. Anything he could do, I could do.

'Mind the broken glass,' he said. He had put his overcoat over the glass on top of the wall, and he moved along to make a space for me, and pulled up his long stockings that had fallen round his ankles, and wriggled himself inside his short trousers.

'I don't usually talk to girls.'

'Why not?'

'Girls are soft.'

'I'm not.'

'You're not a bad climber. For a girl. And a toff,' he said grudgingly.

'Who're you calling a toff?'

'You. You sit all lah-di-dah in that big vicarage and eat banquets off silver plates. All toffs do. And ride round in big cars and tread on the faces of the workers.'

I'm afraid I burst out laughing. Though it was a cold little laugh.

'You'll not laugh when the Red Revolution comes,' he said fiercely. 'We'll string your sort up from lamp posts.'

'*You'd* do that to *me*?'

He gave another grin, with a bit of shame in it. 'Well, not you personally. But the vicar . . . Religion is the opium of the masses.'

'Who says so?'

'My Uncle Henry. He's only a labourer, but he's read Karl Marx.'

'If you only knew,' I said, 'how us toffs *really* live.' And I told him about being so cold all the time.

'By heck,' he said, 'you ought to come to live wi' us workers. Me granda's a retired miner. We're not short of coal. Every time I go to me Nana's I break out into a sweat. Specially today. It's her baking-day. Hey,' he turned to me, 'why don't you come? It's only across the road . . .'

I looked down the other side into a back lane with cricket wickets chalked on the brick walls, every ten yards or so. It didn't seem too hard a drop. I glanced at the gold-plated watch that my father had given me for my last birthday. It was two whole hours until Mrs Brindley would call me for tea. I looked up and caught him looking at my watch, and thinking I was a toff again.

'S'all right. We won't nick your watch. When the Revolution comes, we'll *nationalise* it. All proper and legal . . .'

'Thanks,' I said. 'That's a relief . . .'

'Us workers is honest. Not like the thieving bosses, grinding the faces of the poor.'

'Shut up,' I said. 'Or I'll grind your face personally.'

32

'You don't talk like a girl at all.'
I think he meant it as a compliment.

We walked up the back lane, past women who were gossiping by their gates, their arms entangled with their black shawls. They had very lined faces, and gaps in their teeth as they grinned.

'You courting, young Bobbie?'

'Hallo, hallo, who's your lady-friend?'

Bobbie muttered darkly under his breath. I thought for a moment he was going to take to his heels, and leave me standing there. But he went up to a back gate and opened it, saying:

'This is me Nana's.'

The yard was full of washing, billowing sheets pegged carefully in position so that their snowy white bellies missed touching the sooty brickwork by a fraction of an inch. I edged through them, gingerly; they reached out and enfolded me like clammy ghosts. I was lost in a wilderness of snowy wetness . . .

'Don't touch them,' came Bobbie's muffled voice. 'Your hands'll make them dirty, so she'll have to do them again. Just keep walking.'

I emerged damply from my shroud at last.

'She takes in washing,' said Bobbie, his voice a bit subdued. 'From the toffs. Retired miners don't get much; you have to make ends meet.'

He opened the back door and yelled, 'Yoohoo.'

A yoohoo in reply came from the right. He opened the door and a blast of heat, like a furnace-door being opened, hit me.

The room was lit with a red glow, in which a lot of bits of brass glinted like red jewels. Horse-brasses hung round the kitchen

range; little rows of miniature pots and pans
and windmills on the mantelpiece.

There were great bowls of dough, set to
rise in front of the range. Half the great table
was covered with wire racks of cooling
bread, of all shapes and sizes. The smell was
wonderful.

And on the other half of the table, his Nana
was kneading dough. Great muscular arms
rising and falling, large hands twisting. She
had a powerful beak of a nose, and her dark
hair pulled back in a tight bun, and little
patches of flour on her high forehead. She

gave me a quick look, her hands never stopping. Her small dark eyes missed nothing about my clothes, my watch, the way I stood.

She knew I was a gentry-child, as I knew from the straight-backed way she stood that she had once been a cook in a big house, with a lot of kitchen-maids under her. But she didn't bat an eyelid.

'Won't you sit down, Miss,' she said, very stately and dignified as our cook might have said it. And gave me a wink.

'I'm afraid I'm not one of the workers,' I said. 'I'm just hanging on until the Red Revolution . . .'

She threw back her head and laughed a great laugh. She still had all her own teeth. 'Our Bobbie's got a head full o' rubbish. Our Henry's always filling him wi' daft ideas. Give your guest a plate, our Bobbie. One of the best, the rosebud ones out o' the front room. You'll have a hot bun and butter, Miss, on a cold afternoon like this?'

I sat on her black horsehair sofa and ate a bun, two buns, three buns, dripping with melting butter.

'Set you up,' she said, thumping dough into loaf-shapes, 'for when those Red

Revolutionaries come to chop your head off.
Are you staying somewhere local?'

'The vicarage,' I said, expecting the Ice
Age to descend at any moment.

But she just paused and sighed, and said,
'Oh, that poor man.'

It was the first kind word I'd heard about
my uncle. I was so grateful I could have
wept. She didn't miss that, either.

'It's that Polly Brindley,' she said,
thumping the dough as viciously as she might
have pummelled that lady. 'It's that Polly
Brindley I blame. He was a canny little feller,
your uncle, when he first came. Always gave
you a smile. Till Polly Brindley got her claws
into him. Like she got her claws into the last
vicar. She thinks she runs the parish. Always
coming to the vicarage front door and telling
folks that the vicar isn't in, when he is. Or
the vicar's too busy to bother wi' the likes of
us. She's set people against him something
cruel. And Ah reckon she's on the fiddle at
the corner shop. She buys far more stuff
than one poor man could ever eat . . . still,
that's none o' my business. Another bun,
Miss?'

She went on talking as she worked, and
worked prodigiously. About the old days in

the servants' hall, and the hunt gathering in the park for a stirrup-cup on New Year's morning. I think she told me things she hadn't thought about for thirty years. The time just flew, and our Bobbie listened open-mouthed. It must have been hard for a young Red Revolutionary to take. Then I looked at my watch. It was five minutes to tea-time.

'I must get back,' I said in a panic. 'Thank you for the buns.'

She smiled, a slightly sad smile. 'It's been nice talkin'. Come whenever you like. When you can get. She'll have you cooped up an' all, has she? No going out round the town, mixing wi' the riff-raff?'

'How did you know that?'

'I know my Polly Brindley. I was at school wi' her. She thought she was too good to mix wi' the likes of us, even in those days.'

Bobbie opened the door, and we went into the icy hall. As we stood on the worn doormat, I heard the sound of a racking cough upstairs. Terrible coughing, as if someone was coughing their very soul out.

'Me Granda,' said Bobbie. 'It's the coaldust on his lungs. She has him to see to, an all.'

Then we were running down the lane, to the high wall of the vicarage. Bobbie showed me where to put my feet, where two missing half-bricks made good footholds, and gave me a push on my bum in his turn. I threw down his overcoat, and then we heard the cold hating voice of Polly Brindley calling me from the kitchen door.

'Miss Caroline. Miss *Caroline.*' It wasn't the first time she'd called. She was brewing-up for making a fuss.

'Goodbye,' I whispered. 'Come again.'

'We'll string *her* up from the lamp-post,' he said, 'when the Revolution comes.'

I went back into that cold, cold house.

'You were a long time coming,' said Polly Brindley accusingly.

'I had to tie my shoelaces,' I said.

She sniffed her disbelief.

CHAPTER THREE

Money Matters

Next morning, over breakfast, Uncle Simon
looked up from the dark grey book he was
reading. 'Only a week until Christmas,' he
said, with a weak attempt at a smile. 'I've
been thinking about Christmas. What we
should do, now you've come to spend it with
us. I thought of having a Christmas tree. But
Mrs Brindley has pointed out that they are
heathen things, Christmas trees, and she's
quite right. Heathen things from Germany,
worshipping Odin. Brought over by the late
Prince Consort. Quite wrong in a vicarage.
And their pine needles do make a mess.' He
shuddered delicately, and I knew then that
he was afraid of her. 'Still, we must get you
some presents. But I'm leaving that to the

good offices of Mrs Brindley. I'm sure I don't know what young ladies like for Christmas.'

And he returned to his book, and Christmas seemed already over, shot on the wing before it got to us, like a poor pheasant.

I felt so sick of Mrs Brindley, who came in at that moment to clear the table, and whom I was sure had been eavesdropping at the door, that I grabbed my coat and gloves and went out into the garden, where I could rage in peace.

A pine cone hit me on the ear.

'Don't start *that* again,' I said dangerously.

'Ey,' he said. 'Look what I got for you.' Dangling down the wall, I saw the rustiest old paraffin-stove I had ever seen in my life. The tall cylindrical sort, with three legs.

'We're not a *rubbish*-tip.'

'It works. My dad got it off the tip and mended it. You can have it in the harness-room, to keep you warm. Make a den. Old Brindley will never spot this.'

'*Mrs* Brindley to you.'

'Us workers call her old Brindlebags.'

I couldn't suppress a snigger. He *was* awful.

'Only,' he said, 'it hasn't got no paraffin in it.'

'Well, what good is it?'

'I thought you might have some money . . .' he said longingly.

'How much do you want?'

'Just tuppence. I've got a beer-bottle to carry the paraffin in!'

I reached up and gave it to him, and he vanished.

We sat on old wooden chairs, and stretched out our feet to the stove, which burnt well, in spite of the cracked glass in its window.

'We could brew tea,' he said. 'If we had some tea. Or roast chestnuts, if we had some chestnuts.' He sounded wistful. I couldn't help noticing how thin his legs were. And his shirt collar, though clean, was ragged.

'What does your father do?' I asked.

He said, proudly, 'He's a fitter, a foreman-fitter. He used to build ships. But they don't build ships any more. He's on the dole. But he can do all kinds of things. He can sole and heel shoes and mend bikes and sometimes a car for one of the toffs. We keep going somehow.'

'That's *awful*,' I said.

'Oh, we're lucky. My mam and dad have

only got me; some fellers on the dole have eight or ten kids. They run about in bare feet, even in winter, cos they haven't got no shoes. Everybody's on the dole. But they say, if a war comes . . . there'll be work for everybody again.'

'How awful . . . I don't want there to be a war.'

'A lot of my dad's mates would rather get killed than rot on street corners. That's why there might be a revolution . . .'

'Oh, don't start that again.'

Just at that moment, the cat walked in for her morning scraps. She came as regular as clockwork, now, though Bobbie had never seen her before.

'That's another poor bugger in trouble,' he said gloomily.

'In trouble?'

'Goin' to have kittens. Any minute now. Don't they teach you nothin' at your public school?'

'*We* only have dogs,' I said, a bit snootily.

'For chasing poor bloody foxes with . . .'

But I didn't rise to his bait. I was too worried about the cat.

'She can't have kittens here. It's too cold.'

'Reckon she hasn't got anywhere else to

go. She's flipping starving.'

'But why hasn't she got a home? She's so tame.' The cat finished her bacon rind and came and rubbed against my hand for more.

'People chuck them out, 'cos they can't afford to feed them. Lot of people drown them. Put them in a sack and chuck them in the river. River's full of 'em.'

The cat rubbed against my hand, and looked at me, trusting, confiding.

And suddenly it wasn't a matter of kindness to animals any more; it was a matter of life and death. She was just as much in need of love as our dogs at home.

'This is *intolerable*,' I stormed.

'Ye'll just have to learn that's the way things are round here. We have to put up wi' it. There's little bairns starvin', let alone cats.'

'We must do *something*. Can't *you* take her home?'

'We gotta dog already, an' we can hardly feed that. Only the butcher gives me mam free bones, and she boils them for soup, then the dog has them afterwards.'

'What about your Nana?' I thought of that stout determined redoubtable woman.

'She's got two cats already. She couldn't cope with six more.'

'*Six*?'

'The kittens, stupid. Kittens grow up to be cats.'

'I could give her money for them . . .'

He gave a look that was suddenly cold, remote. 'We divven't accept charity.'

'Sorry,' I said. 'It's just that I'm scared Mrs Brindley will find out . . . she'd have them destroyed. She can twist my uncle round her little finger.'

'Aye,' he said bitterly. 'Reckon she'd have poor people destroyed if she could. When the Revolution . . .'

'Shut *up!*'

There was a long silence. After a while he said, 'I could build her a hiding-place. To have the kittens in.'

He got up, and rooted around the harness-room. Got an old thick cardboard box, that said 'Carnation Milk, One Gross'. He went out to the stable, and came back with it half-full of clean crumpled hay. Then he folded the lid cleverly, leaving only a small hole in the top. Put it back against the wall, under the big table one used for cleaning harness. Laid one or two old planks of wood and an empty paint-tin on top.

His hands were clever. It was a good hiding-place, warm and dark, and no one would ever think of looking inside it, it looked so normal, boring. He gently picked the cat up and showed the box to her, let her sniff it. Then popped her inside. We listened to her rustling about in the hay, pounding it with her paws. Then she poked her head up through the hole, and sat looking at us with such a comical expression of triumph on her face.

'She's tekken to it,' he said, in a voice of low glad glee. 'She'll have her kittens in there now.'

'If only the kittens don't cry out!'

'They'll knaa enough to keep their mouths shut, when the Brindley's prowling round.'

'You make her sound like a tiger or a wolf or something!'

'Aye,' he said grimly.

'There's one more thing worrying me. I'm stealing scraps from the table to feed her. If Mrs Brindley catches me . . .'

'Goodbye scraps. And goodbye cat . . .'

'Oh, don't worry,' I said loftily. 'I can tell a lie. I can lie as well as anybody when I want to. She won't find out about the cat. But I won't be able to come here any more – she'll be watching me like a hawk. Will you go on feeding the cat?'

'What with?' He shrugged, looking down at his feet, ashamed of his poverty and helplessness. 'She can't eat grass, you knaa.'

'I'll give you money to buy things. I've got plenty of money.' I reached into my purse and pulled out the five pound note that Daddy had sent me for the Christmas holidays. They were huge plain white things in those days.

'What the hell's that?' he asked. 'Your school report?'

'Five pound note.'

He took it from me and examined it closely; crinkled it between his fingers, smelt it, like a little animal. Then he gave it back quickly. The shine went out of his eyes; they went as dull as ditchwater.

'If the feller at the corner shop saw me wi' a *ten-shilling* note, he'd send for the poliss.'

'But it's all I've got,' I said, tears of frustration seeping into the corners of my eyes. 'Except two sixpences.'

'Ah can do a lot wi' a sixpence . . .'

'No,' I said. 'I'll go to the bank and change it. What kind of money do you need?'

'Nothing bigger than a two-shilling bit,' he said.

'We'd better go now,' I said. 'Before it

gets dark. It's an hour till tea-time yet.'

'C'mon then. Ah'll show you the sights o' Shields. Bring on the dancing girls . . .'

You cannot imagine, granddaughter, the sights I saw that day. Groups of unemployed men, squatting at the street corners, passing round the flattened dog-end of a cigarette from one to the other; smoking it, with the aid of a pin stuck through it until it was only a quarter inch-long. A man with no legs, just flat worn black leather pads where his legs should be, singing carols in a deep sweet voice from a doorstep, with his little dog nearby and a flat cap into which some passers-by put halfpennies.

But in the end we reached the bank, with its tall sandstone columns.

'You're never going in *there*,' whispered Bobbie, awe-struck.

'Why not?' I said. 'It's *my* money.'

And I sailed in, as I often had before, and the man behind the counter not only changed the note exactly as I asked, but called me 'Madam' of course. What was the difference between me and Bobbie, I wondered? I wasn't dressed grandly, I can tell you. Only a sensible country tweed coat and hat. But I

suppose my voice was what Bobbie would have called posh. And the man behind the counter was my servant; I expected him to obey, and he did. With a little subservient smirk. I had a brief thought about Bobbie and his Red Revolution . . . were Red Revolutions infectious? The man behind the counter wouldn't like a Red Revolution at all. The workers would probably string him up from the nearest lamp-post. Before helping themselves to his bank . . .

When I got outside, Bobbie caught my arm.

'We'll have to run like hell,' he said.

'Why, for heavens sake?'

'It's starting to rain . . . Brindley'll be out in the garden looking for you in a minute.'

I have never run so fast in my life.

Bobbie gave me a last heave up on to the wall, and I listened in the growing dusk. The vicarage lights were on, and the rain was now falling steadily.

'You got that money safe?' I whispered down to him.

'Yeah,' he whispered back. 'Best of British luck wi' Brindley.'

Then I was dropping down into the wet garden, and he was gone. I felt very alone. But rather excited. Like a spy. I listened more carefully. No sound of Brindlebags calling for me; that was bad. That meant she'd been calling and given up. Maybe she had even searched the garden for me, and not found me. Still, I walked round to the front door, sauntering along as if I didn't have a care in the world. As luck would have it, I met my uncle as he came through the gate.

'Caroline,' he said, 'what are you doing out in this rain?'

'Oh,' I said gaily, 'I sheltered in the old hayloft. It's quite dry up there.' How easy it is, to lie.

'I hope you looked where you were going,' he said. 'They say the hayloft floor is rotten in places . . .'

Just then, Mrs Brindley opened the front door.

'Where have you been, you wicked girl! I've looked everywhere for you. You were nowhere to be found . . .'

I remembered the bank, where the man had been my servant. Mrs Brindley was also a servant, though she had long since forgotten her place.

'Oh,' I said, in a voice of disgust, 'I heard you calling. I'm sick of you calling for me. Like I was a pet dog. Or a cow.'

'Caroline!' said my uncle, in a very shocked voice. Adamsons are *never* rude to their servants. It might have gone hard with me; if Mrs Brindley hadn't forgotten herself again, and been ruder back.

'She's lying. I looked everywhere.'

'Up in the hayloft?' I asked sweetly, looking up and down her massive fat body. 'How many rungs are missing on the ladder?'

She knew she was beaten there; she shot me a look of pure hatred. But she wouldn't give up. She turned to my uncle. 'She's so

disobedient. I can't be expected to take responsibility . . .'

'I can be responsible for myself,' I said stoutly. 'I *am* nearly twelve years old . . .'

For the first time, I saw a flicker of fear in her piggy little eyes.

'Come, come now,' said my poor uncle, all atremble, 'let us have peace and harmony. This is a Christian household. I want a word with you in my study, Caroline.'

Mrs Brindley smirked and left, quite sure she had won. I followed my uncle into his cold study, with its poor, smoking fire. How different from Bobbie's Nana's generous blaze. And the hearth hadn't been swept properly. There was a rim of ash half-hidden behind the fender, half-an-inch high. Mrs Brindley was a slut into the bargain.

My uncle sat down, his pale podgy hands clasped between his black thighs.

'Caroline,' he said, as severely as he could muster, 'you know what I am going to say to you . . .'

'She called me a liar,' I said coldly. 'She is a *servant*, and she called me a liar. What do you think my father is going to say about *that*?'

Poor weak man, how we tormented him,

Mrs Brindley and I between us. He wrung his hands, and did not know what to say.

Except, 'Is there no peace in this world?'

I wondered then what God thought of me; for God was very close and real to me in those days. And then I thought of God's cat, God's creature that Mrs Brindley would destroy if she could.

'She is over-familiar,' I said. 'She has got above herself.' I thought of all the other things I might have said; the grocer's bill, the filthy fireplace. But I was only a child; he would not have taken it from me.

'She has so much to do,' he said. 'It makes her over-hasty. But she means it for the best.' Poor fool. I made up my mind then that I would destroy Mrs Brindley. But I just said, 'Very well, uncle. I will try to be civil to her,' and got up and went to the door.

'There was one more thing,' he said, with a little shy, timid smile, staring at something over my shoulder. 'Miss Stevenson – my organist – has sent to say she is unwell and unable to play for daily evensong. I was wondering if you would come and sing it with me?'

'With all my heart,' I said, and meant it. It was a way of saying sorry to God.

CHAPTER FOUR

A Game of Spies

He lifted the heavy latch, and the metallic clink echoed up and down the dark empty church. The stained-glass angels of the windows were pointed islands of dim light in the blackness.

'Wait here,' said my uncle, 'while I put on the lights.' He walked into the darkness ahead, where only a tiny red flame flickered high up in the sanctuary lamp; red as blood. His footsteps were sure and confident, as if he knew the way by heart.

Then the chancel lights came on, dimly golden, and he was taking off his dark overcoat, and slipping on his white surplice.

'You know the service?'

'We sing it every Sunday in school chapel.'

'Good girl. Do you think you can manage without the organ? It's a good church for singing in. Fine echo!'

'I can try!'

'Good girl!' he said again.

And it worked. He was a singer, and I was a singer, and the dark aisles and pillars of the church took us up and echoed us as if they were a whole multitude. We made the stones ring into the very far corners, where the cobwebs hung and the mice ran. There is no feeling like that.

'O Lord, open Thou our lips!'

'And our mouths shall shew forth Thy Praise!'

'O Lord, make speed to save us!'

'O Lord, make haste to help us!'

I sang like an angel, and plotted like a devil. The downfall of Mrs Brindley. I could not think what God must have thought.

We came to an end and stopped. Uncle Simon buried his face in his hands in prayer, and I pretended to do the same, but watched him through my spread fingers. He seemed to be praying an awfully long time, even for a vicar. And then I noticed that his back was heaving, as it only heaves when somebody is laughing or crying.

I knew my uncle would never laugh in church. I was left with the terrible knowledge that one of my grown-ups was crying.

And a man at that. I had sometimes seen my mother cry, though not often, and usually about the death of a beloved dog. I had never seen my father cry; though if a favourite dog had died, the muscles of his cheeks twitched very fiercely, and he chewed savagely at the ends of his grey moustache.

I walked over to Uncle Simon, cautiously. I was a little afraid, and yet I felt a power; or the beginnings of a power. I touched him on the shoulder, gently. 'Uncle?'

He raised a face wet with tears, and yet twisted with shame that I should see him thus.

'It was so beautiful,' he said. 'The singing.'

I nodded, not knowing what to say.

'It seemed so *right*.'

I nodded again.

'It always seems right in church. Yet the moment I go outside . . .' He looked round the church, as if desperately seeking an answer. 'They are a hard-hearted people. They have hardened their hearts against me . . .'

'There *are* some good people,' I said. Thinking of Bobbie with the cat, and his Nana looking after the whole family.

'How can *you* know, child? You haven't been among them!'

Suddenly his eyes were very sharp, even through their tears. I had nearly fallen into a snare. But I said quickly, 'There are good people everywhere.'

'True,' he said. 'Out of the mouths of babes and sucklings . . . Then it is *my* fault . . . Some did smile at me when I first came. There were people came to church, then . . .'

I took a deep breath and said, 'I don't think it's *your* fault.'

His eyes clung to mine, like a drowning man clings to a straw.

'*She* turns people away. From the vicarage door.'

Again, his eyes went sharper. 'How do you know that, child?'

'She turned me away. She didn't know who I was, but she turned me away. She didn't even ask what I wanted. I could have been someone whose mother was dying or *anything*.'

'She apologized for that; she had

something in the oven and was afraid it was going to burn. You mustn't make mountains out of molehills, Caroline. But,' he got up, 'thank you for bearing with me. I feel better now.' And the vagueness came back over his eyes, and I knew my chance was gone.

For the moment.

I knew she was looking for an opportunity to spy on me; so the next morning I gave it to her. For the cat's sake, the sooner it was over, the better. I laid a trap for her; I went out on a morning when even I might have lurked indoors, a morning with a steel-grey sky and biting wind. It was two days to Christmas.

I had a cold hour of it, crouching in the rhododendron bushes that overlooked the back door. I think I must have turned blue with cold; I almost despaired.

And then I saw the back door cautiously open, and her head come out, and look left and right. Then the whole bulk of her was tiptoeing in among the trees. It was ridiculous, the care she took; and yet she was so clumsy she made more noise than a herd of elephants. At least, in future, I knew what kind of noise to listen for.

What games I had with her; following her ten yards behind, mimicking her rolling waddling gait, until I had to stuff my hanky in my mouth to stop myself giggling out loud. (Like any fool, she never looked *behind*.) I picked up pine cones and threw them to left and right, making her jump with the small rustlings and crashes. Oh, such a game. And then, when she was at the far end of the garden from the stable, and bent almost double to peer under a monkey puzzle tree, with her great rump in the air, I crept across the silent pine needles and poked her in the bum and shouted loudly, 'Boo!'

She jumped a foot in the air; whirled with her hand at her throat, as if she was about to have a heart attack.

'Oh, Miss Caroline,' she blustered, when she got her breath back. 'You gave me such a turn.'

'Were you looking for me?' I asked mock-sweetly. 'Was there something you wanted?'

'I just wanted to know if you could do wi' a hot drink. It's such a parky morning.'

'That's very sweet of you.'

She smirked. Then I added, 'I've been following you for ten minutes. You were

trying to *spy* on me.'

All pretence of sweetness fled. She gave me such a look of hatred that even I recoiled. I suppose even stupid people hate being caught out in their stupidity.

'You're up to some game, Miss,' she said, 'and I'll find you out. I know what you're up to.'

'And I know what you're up to,' I said.

'What *do* you mean?' She drew herself up to a great height, though her little piggy eyes flickered.

'I know what you get up to at the corner shop. Buying too much.' I suppose I meant to *really* frighten her; to frighten her away from me altogether. Blackmail, I suppose.

But it didn't work. If she'd hated me before, she only hated me more now. Some people are so stupid they have no sense of their own good at all.

'You think you're so *clever*,' she spat. 'But I'll settle your hash, missie, you see if I don't.' And then she stalked off back to the house.

I knew she would never spy on me in the garden again. What I didn't grasp was that the garden was my territory, where I had the advantage. The house was hers.

I slid carefully into the harness-room. The gentle smell of burning paraffin told me Bobbie was there. There was a second object burning paraffin now; an incredibly battered old hurricane lamp hung from a long nail, casting a soft yellow light.

Bobbie was kneeling on the floor, beside the cardboard box. He looked up, his grin enormous, his blue eyes shining as they had never done before. It might have been Christmas morning.

'They've come,' he said. 'They've come. Three of them.'

'Who?' I asked stupidly, still full of the bitterness of my quarrel.

'The *kittens*. I watched them being born. An hour ago. They came in little shiny sacks, like cellophane, on the end of little strings. She chewed them out of the sacks. I was so scared. I thought she was eatin' them. Then she licked them dry, all over. And now they're feedin off her. All purrin' their heads off. I *wish* you'd been here. It was marvellous.'

I suppose it should have taught me a lesson. I'd been so busy feeding my hate that I'd missed all the glory. Though of course I had seen puppies born, and I don't suppose

65

kittens are much different . . .

'Come and see.' His voice was low and reverent, as if he was in church. And there they lay, on the hay, between their mother's outstretched legs. Climbing and pummelling with their tiny paws and treading in each other's faces; and sucking and purring at the same time like tiny bees. One all black one, one nearly all white, with black spots, and one ginger and black.

'I think I know the dad,' said Bobbie. 'Mrs Haggerty's ginger tom. He's a crafty old sod.' He picked one up, and showed it to me, cupping it ever so gently in the palm of his hands. It was the little ginger one. Its ears were crumpled like rose petals, its eyes bulged blindly behind closed slits.

Its ginger paws flailed frantic and blind, clawing the air to find a mother who had inexplicably vanished, and it squeaked piteously.

I had never seen anything so vulnerable; to come into this cruel hard world. My heart was a torrent of love. I vowed I would do murder to save it.

'Put it back,' I cried. 'Give it back to its mother. It'll catch a chill.' It was *unbearable*.

He laughed, not unkindly. 'Don't you worry; it's a tough little sod. See how it kicks!' Then he saw the look on my face, and put it back. Quickly, it snuggled back in between its siblings, and all was purring and sucking again.

'Got anything to eat?' he asked. 'The mother's ravenous. I managed to nick some bacon-rind from me dad's tea, but it was gone in a flash. Like feeding an elephant strawberries.'

I got out my little bag of scraps, and offered them to the mother. She sniffed at them, then stirred uneasily, torn between the food and the kittens. I put the bits on the hay beside her and she got upright, the protesting kittens still trying to cling to her belly, then falling away, and squealing loudly.

She ate; she was wolfish, and yet with every bite, her ears swivelled to the kittens' protests. She was so frantic, my heart went out to her, too.

When she had finished, and all the uproar was over, and the kittens and cat settled in a purring mass again. I said,

'You'd better start buying her food. I can't smuggle out enough for her.'

'That's O.K. I found out when the cat's meat man comes round with his barrow. I'll meet him down the town, where nobody will recognize me.' I grinned at him. He had to act like a spy too, now. He had nosy grown-ups to dodge as well. I thought he'd make a good spy.

Then I got up. I was very tense. On the one hand were the helpless kittens; on the other, the prowling hating Mrs Brindley. She would still be watching for me, out of the house windows . . .

'See you tomorrow,' I said.

'Same time, eh?' he grinned. 'I'll bring a bottle of water too. She's thirsty.'

'Milk would be better . . .'

'I'll get a gill o' milk. Me Nana's got a little chipped jug she won't miss for a bit . . .'

I think I fell in love with him then. With his

toughness and reliability.

Oh, yes, granddaughter. You can fall in love when you're not quite twelve. With the most unsuitable people.

One day to Christmas.

It was at breakfast that disaster struck. I suppose I was too eager to nick the scraps off the plates. My uncle had left a fine big piece of ham fat on the edge of his, and had pushed it idly across the breakfast-table towards me, lost in his book. I thought I was safe. I could have pinched the tablecloth itself, when he was lost in his book. He would merely have lifted his elbows to let me take it . . .

But I didn't hear Mrs Brindley come in through the door to clear up. She might have been noisy in the garden, but in the house she could move as silently as a mouse, in her old carpet-slippers. Too late, I heard the soft creak of her corset stays, and then she cried loudly.

'What are you doing with that ham fat, Miss? Don't we feed you well enough?'

My uncle looked up, bewildered, to see the large lump of ham fat in my hand.

'She was going to slip it into her cardigan

pocket, sir. Look, the edge of her pocket's all greasy . . . what's this, then?' She plunged her great paw into my pocket, and flourished my bag of scraps in triumph under my poor uncle's nose.

'Caroline?' he said.

'She's a-feeding something, sir. Stealing food to feed something. I know her little ways.'

'*Are* you feeding something, Caroline?' asked my uncle, with mild interest.

God, my mind was in a whirl. Could I pretend I was feeding some poor stray dog, that came to the gate? But the gate was always shut. Could I pretend I was indeed half-starved? But I had left a lump of bread and butter on my side plate . . .

'Caroline, *please* give me an answer,' said my uncle, starting to get a little cross, while Mrs Brindley breathed heavily through her mouth in triumphant righteousness.

Then a vision of our garden at home came to my rescue in a nick of time.

'Tits,' I said.

'I *beg* your pardon?' said my uncle, very shocked.

I had a ridiculous desire to giggle at his pious, shocked face. But I controlled myself, and said, with an effort, 'Blue-tits, great-tits, coal-tits. They love fat. And it's the winter, and they're so *hungry* . . .'

My uncle's face cleared. 'There's nothing to be ashamed of in that. St Francis *preached* to the birds, Mrs Brindley. If we can't feed our feathered friends in winter . . . But there was no need to be underhand, Caroline. If you'd asked, I'm sure Mrs

Brindley would have found you lots of bits for the birds.'

'Ain't no birds in this garden, sir. I've looked many a time. She's feedin' something a lot bigger than a bird . . .'

My uncle looked torn both ways. In a moment, Mrs Brindley was going to win. A vision of the cat and kittens swam up in front of my eyes. Living. Dead. Drowned. Mrs Brindley would certainly know a man prepared to drown them; if she didn't take satisfaction in drowning them herself.

'Come and see,' I said. 'They come for me every morning. Down by the gate.' I said the gate, because the only birds I had ever seen in North Shields were sparrows, pecking their breakfasts in the mats of flattened horse-dung on the roads. But a sparrow was better than nothing . . .

We all trooped down. It would have looked ridiculous, if it hadn't been a matter of life and death. I scattered the pieces, the precious pieces, on the weedy drive, and we retired to a distance and waited.

Nothing came. We got very cold. My uncle began to fidget. Mrs Brindley's stertorious breathing got more and more triumphant. While I humbly prayed.

Anything with wings, please God. Pigeons, vultures . . . Anything at all.

'Nothing,' said Mrs Brindley, at last. 'I told you, sir. No birds in . . .'

And at that moment, a solitary starling, black as soot with the smoke of the town, fluttered down. Then two more, then two more. A whole crowd, as starlings do. *Blessed* starlings; blessed, dirty starlings.

'There,' I said, when they had finished the scraps and flown away again.

'I'm not sure they're t . . . blue-tits,' said my uncle doubtfully. 'But I was never one for nature-study. However, if you *ask* Mrs Brindley, Caroline, I'm sure she will lay on plenty of scraps for you in the future.'

He walked off back to his study, leaving us glaring at each other.

I knew I mustn't go to the stables any more. Our margin of safety was now as thin as paper.

CHAPTER FIVE

Double Visions

All I could do was wander round the other bits of the garden disconsolately. I knew Bobbie would twig something was wrong eventually.

I was right. After two weary hours, a pine cone hit me on the ear. It was very welcome.

We hid deep in the rhododendrons, while I told him what had happened. He considered carefully. Then he said, 'She's only watching you. She doesn't know about me, right? So I can keep on feeding the cat. She's all right – I got a huge load off the cat-meat man for a penny. She ate the lot. She's got milk, too.'

'Bless you. But Brindlebags mustn't see you . . .'

'She won't. I can get over the wall, right next to the stables. Lots of bricks are loose, I can make new footholds.'

As I said, he would have made a good spy.

Then he shuffled uncomfortably. 'Can I ask you a favour? There's a little girl lives next door to us. She's got TB – consumption. She hasn't got no toys, they're that hard-up. I go in to play with her sometimes, to cheer her up. She gets that bored . . . well, I told her about the kittens coming.'

'Oh, how *could* you?' I was furious. 'It was a *secret*.'

'It's still a secret, don't you worry. She knows how to keep her mouth shut. So do her parents. And nobody talks to the vicar or Mrs Brindley – they wouldn't tell her the time o' day. We're quite safe, only . . .'

'Only *what*?'

'She wants to see the kittens.'

'NO!'

He was silent, for a long time. Then he said, 'She won't make old bones, little Shirley. Me mam doubts she'll last out the winter. Says she'll be gone by spring, like the birds.'

'But how can she see them, if she's that

ill?' I was still angry with him, but I was melting, under his serious gaze.

'Her mam lets her out to play, when it's not raining. If she's well wrapped-up. We push her about in an old push-chair. She's sort of the mascot of our gang . . .'

'But how will you get her over the wall?'

'Our gang will help. Two at the bottom of the wall, and two at the top, wi' a bit o' rope. They're strong lads. We'll manage easy. We'll wait till it starts getting dark. Nobody will see us, honest. We nick the vicar's apples off his trees in summer, and nobody ever sees us then.'

'Thanks very much! I hadn't realised you were a *criminal* gang.'

But I couldn't resist his earnestness. Or the thought of little Shirley. I would still be alive next summer.

'Do as you like,' I said. 'You won't see me for a bit. I'm going to stay indoors and annoy the Brindlebags. That'll take her mind off the stables.'

And I walked away, still in a huff. Why couldn't I belong to a gang like that?

It began to snow that afternoon. Big soft flakes whirling down past the library window, as I shivered and tried to read a boring book about Christianity and the unemployed. It was full of ideas about how Christianity could help the unemployed. Setting up soup kitchens and Christian reading rooms for the men. But that was in London. It didn't seem to be happening in North Shields . . .

I heard the front door open, and Uncle Simon come in. He looked in at the library door. He had a lot of holly and mistletoe in his arms, and looked more cheerful than usual.

'The Great Feast of Christmas is about to begin,' he said.

Then Mrs Brindley came bustling out, and began to grumble about what a bother putting up holly and mistletoe was, and had the vicar got any drawing pins, for you couldn't put up holly and mistletoe without them, and there were certainly none in the house . . .

That wiped all the cheerfulness off Uncle Simon's face. We'd probably never even see the holly and mistletoe. It would probably just get pushed around the kitchen table until it withered and died. I did offer to go to the corner shop for some drawing pins, saying the corner shop sold everything . . . But Mrs Brindley just asked in a nasty voice how I knew about the corner shop, and I had to shut up. Uncle Simon wouldn't have let me out into the godless town anyway.

The next morning, the snow was lying all about, deep and crisp and even. I almost hated it. It ruled out any chance of going up to see the kittens. Footsteps that led anywhere near the stables would be fatal. I just hoped cat, kittens and Bobbie were doing all right; and annoyed Mrs Brindley by offering to help put up the holly. I could tell she was a bit baffled at my staying indoors.

She kept on hinting that I should go out and make a snowman or something. But I wasn't falling for that one, and just said snow was cold nasty stuff, and I *really* hated it.

There was only one consolation. My uncle insisted that she light a fire for me in the library; whether because he'd finally realised I was cold, or merely because it was Christmas Eve, it was impossible to say. She responded with a smouldering mountain of coal dust in the grate, that never showed a flicker of flame all day, however I poked and coaxed it that sent a cloud of choking smoke across the shelves of old books, every time the wind blew a fresh flurry of flakes against the windows.

I tried to forget myself in an uplifting book, full of death-bed conversions of wicked sinners. But my eyes were constantly drawn to the windows, with their view of the roof of the distant stables. How was the cat doing? Had her supply of milk dried up with the cold? Had the kittens frozen to death? Had Bobbie managed to get food in to them? Had he brought Shirley to see them yet? Several times Mrs Brindley, coming in quietly, nearly caught me staring at the stables. Even when your father was flying jet-fighters, granddaughter, I never knew such maternal worry.

But in the end the weary day passed, and darkness fell, and it was time for my uncle's return, and tea. He bustled into the library, rosy-cheeked with the cold, and unwound his enormously long scarf; but I noticed he was too wise to take his overcoat off, and he grumbled a little about the fire. Then Mrs Brindley bustled in with the tray; my uncle had laid on muffins to mark the occasion, but she had managed to burn them all round the edges. She went across to draw the curtains against the night. Then she stopped halfway, and said, in a dreadful doom-laden voice,

'There is someone in the stables! I can see a light!'

'Nonsense,' said my uncle, a little grumpily, reaching for a muffin. 'What would anyone want in our old stables?'

'Trespassers. Hooligans. Thieves,' screeched Mrs Brindley. 'They will burn the place down.'

My uncle went to the window grudgingly; I think he only meant to shut her up. And I followed him with a sinking heart.

There was a light in the lower window of the stables, showing through the trunks of the trees. Only a dim light; but as we looked, it winked, as if someone had walked across it. I cursed Bobbie in my heart, for his stupidity.

'We must ring for the police,' screeched Mrs Brindley.

'I will see to it myself,' said my uncle, huffily. He wound on his scarf again, with a deep long-suffering sigh, and set out followed by Mrs Brindley breathing fire and thunder.

'Be silent, woman,' said my uncle, 'or they will hear you and escape.' It worked; nothing else would have silenced her. I had managed to slip between them.

Our approach was quite noiseless through the snow . . .

You may wonder why I did not cry out a warning. But that would have betrayed my own position completely, and I still hoped to help somehow . . .

The silence inside the stable was absolute as well. Perhaps Bobbie had gone; perhaps the light was only the light of the stove left burning for the cats . . .

My uncle flung wide the door.

And it was then that God played one of his little jokes. Or it may have been purely an

accident. I have never, all my life, been able
to separate God's little jokes from accidents,
granddaughter.

The scene inside the stable was the scene
of the Nativity; by the red glow of the
paraffin stove, and the dim golden light of the
hurricane lamp, it was exactly the scene on
all the Christmas cards my uncle sent out.

Not just the stable, with the straw on the
floor, and the disused manger. But Mary
was there kneeling in the straw, with her
blue-clad arms round the new baby. And the
ragged, tousle-haired shepherds knelt
beside her in adoration, and on her left, the
three kings stood, black Balthasar, crowned
and splendid in red and gold, and oriental

Melchior, with his calm face and blue garb, and flaxen-haired Caspar. And behind Mary, brooding, protective, stood Joseph. And all eyes were fixed in silent worship . . .

And then Mrs Brindley cried, 'Thieves, hooligans,' and the children looked up startled, and King Balthasar was simply a black boy in a red and yellow bobble hat and jumper and scarf, and Mary only Shirley, a pale little girl with huge scared blue eyes and a blue overcoat with its hood up, and St Joseph was only Bobbie, with a sack draped round his back to keep out the cold, and a rough stick in his hand, and the baby was only a startled she-cat at bay, spitting in defence of her helpless mewing kittens, who sprawled in the straw.

'Fetch the poliss,' cried Mrs Brindley.

But my uncle stood as if transfixed, with the tears running down his pale fat cheeks, and I knew he had seen with my eyes, not Mrs Brindley's.

He cried out, in agony, 'Suffer the little children to come unto me, for such is the kingdom of heaven!'

'I'll run for the poliss, Reverend!' shouted Mrs Brindley.

'Shut *up*, you stupid woman,' shouted my

uncle.

'I'm not standing here listening to that kind of talk,' shouted Mrs Brindley.

'Then *go*,' shouted my uncle.

And all the children just stood, open-mouthed, wide-eyed, paralysed with amazement that such things should be.

Then my uncle was among the children, shaking them by the hand one by one, babbling strange and discordant jollities.

'You must come into the house. We shall have mince pies! Ginger ale! Jellies!' He must have been lost in some distant dream of his own happy childhood. 'Come, down to the house. You are all welcome, most welcome.'

The children were torn between acceptance and flight, at such an unlikely jovial madman.

They all looked at Bobbie. He was the leader. He thought hard, narrowing his shrewd young eyes, weighing up the situation. Then he nodded; and they all trailed after the vicar. For in that town of cold and hunger and unemployment, the promise of *anything* to eat was the kingdom of heaven.

The she-cat was busy carrying her off-

spring back into their box, wise and prudent mother that she was. I saw her safe in, and doused the lights for fear of fire, and then ran to join the rest.

I found them huddled in the hall. My uncle was shouting at Mrs Brindley again. 'Bring ginger ale, Mrs Brindley! Warm the mince pies!'

'We haven't got none. You didn't ask me to get any in . . . you can't expect a hardworking housekeeper to . . .'

'Surely we have *something*? Christmas cake, seedy-cake, anything!'

'Only your dinner tomorrow . . .'

'We *must* have something . . .'

'Don't talk to me like that, Vicar. I think you've taken leave of your senses . . . I will not stay one minute longer and be shouted at like that. I'm giving in my notice, as of now.'

And good as her word, she took her coat off the hook on the back of the kitchen door, and swept away without another word, slamming the front door behind her.

I never heard a sweeter sound. But there was a sudden horrible silence, in which hope faded from the children's faces as the real world returned, and visions of Christmas plenty died. And my poor uncle, flapped his hands helplessly, saying over and over again,

'What shall I do? What *shall* I do? What shall I do now?'

Mrs Brindley might still have won then. But Bobbie seized his chance. He stepped forward, and stood to attention before my uncle, like a soldier.

'I can get them for you, sir! The corner shop has plenty of drink, mince pies.'

'Splendid chap,' my uncle clapped him on the shoulder, 'off you go then . . .'

Bobbie hesitated beautifully; I have never seen the late Laurence Olivier do it better.

'Oh, yes, money, money, you need money,' said my uncle fumbling up under the long skirt of his cassock and revealing a perfectly ordinary pair of dark trousers, much to the children's amazement.

He produced a very crumpled pound note. 'Here you are!' The children's eyes widened, as at all the treasures of the Spanish Main.

'Here, better have two,' said my uncle, adding another note to the first. The children looked as if paradise was assured. Bobbie and his black friend sped off like the wind.

CHAPTER SIX

Merry Christmas

It was a marvellous party, all the better for being straight out of bottles, packets and tins. There should have been crumbs all over the library carpet; but these were children who pursued crumbs and picked them up with the ends of their fingers, and ate them. Afterwards, the vicar thumped away on the old piano like one possessed and we sang carols till our throats were sore. For they knew all the carols by heart, from school, even the Chinese boy, whose name I learnt was, amazingly, Ted Mulligan.

At last, when we could eat no more and sing no more, the vicar led them down to the front gate, pressing on them whatever had not already been eaten, for their parents and brothers and sisters. There were about thirty children by that time, for word had spread round quickly from Joe's Corner Shop that the vicar was holding a children's Christmas party, and disbelief had been overcome by hunger, and many had knocked on the door and been let in afterwards.

'Good night, good night,' called Uncle Simon, delirious with glee. 'Merry Christmas to you all, and to your parents.'

Now it just happened that a lot of grown-ups were passing the gate at the time, having been out to do what little Christmas shopping they could afford. I heard them muttering to each other, at the strange sight of the vicarage gate open, and happy children streaming out.

'My God, the vicar's been holding a Christmas party!'

'Wonders never cease! They'll be doubling the dole next!'

Then an adult voice called, back over its shoulder, 'Merry Christmas, Vicar!'

And all the rough adult voices were calling.

'Merry Christmas, Reverend!'

God's little joke, or the accident, was continuing.

We went back indoors, to the litter of bags and boxes and bottles on every chair and table.

'Oh dear,' said my uncle, his face suddenly falling. 'Whatever shall we do now? However can we *cope?*' He had the petulant baby look of a helpless male suddenly left to manage alone.

I knew he'd *never* manage alone. Over the days, once I was gone, the need for Mrs Brindley would come drifting back. The need to have his meals cooked, his socks darned, his shirts washed . . . inexorable. Mrs Brindley could win yet; and extract a terrible vengeance.

So I took a deep breath, and cut Mrs Brindley's throat for good and all. I was never sure whether that was part of God's little joke or not.

'I know a good woman who could do for you,' I said.

'A *respectable* woman?' A look of fright crossed his face.

'A respectable woman,' I said, 'and a very respectable cook. She used to work in a big house as cook, when she was younger . . .'

His eyes lit up; he was always a bit of a glutton. And I ran to Bobbie's Nana's, before he could stop me. God knows how I found the right gate in the dark. But she came, all flustered, with her hair hastily screwed up in a new bun, and a spotless white apron under her best hat and coat.

He never looked back after that. At Midnight Mass that Christmas Eve, where I had expected a dreary congregation of three, we had nearly twenty. More than for years . . . word got around fast in that town. The parents of the children from the party, mainly.

And after that, with Bobbie's Nana to take him in hand, and answer his front door, and guide him with her sound common sense, his congregation grew. The next Christmas Eve, the church was nearly full; even if some of them were more than a little drunk, including my old unbuttoned friend, still grieving for his black sins.

As for Bobbie, I didn't see him again for years, after that second Christmas Eve. But I heard about his progress from my uncle. How his father got new work, as the Second World War drew nearer; building destroyers to sink U-boats. So that they could afford to send Bobbie to grammar school after all. How he was top of his class, and got all his exams. How he joined the RAF.

But it was not until 1945, April 1945, that he came walking up our drive one fine evening, when I happened to be on leave from the Wrens. He was wearing the wings of a navigator, and his left arm was in a black silk sling, and I'm afraid I didn't recognize him at first. He had grown into a very attractive young man. Not good-looking, but snub-nosed still, with warm blue eyes, and a wicked grin.

'Why didn't you look us up earlier,' I cried.

'Not till I'd done something worthwhile,' he grinned.

'Like getting yourself nearly killed?'

'And I'm still only a flight-sergeant, and you're a flipping officer . . .'

It was as if I had just left him yesterday.

'Are you going to take me out to dinner?' I asked. I was always very forward, granddaughter.

'I haven't been to university yet,' he said grimly, almost to himself.

'Oh, I can't wait till you get your degree,' I said.

And we took it on from there.

Look at him now, weeding that rockery. You've guessed, haven't you, the famous Bobbie. Grey as a badger now, though it suits him. And he's still got his snub nose and wicked grin . . .

You wouldn't be here, if I hadn't been hit on the ear by a pine cone, in that horrible dark vicarage garden, all those years ago.

The cats? That vicarage was always famous for its cats. That's one of their descendants, asleep in that chair.

Beware of pine cones, granddaughter.